PENELOPE MILLER was born and brought up in Farlington, Portsmouth. Spending many years in Cornwall, she has now returned to Gosport, Hampshire, to be near her three children and seven grandchildren.

Now retired, she likes nothing more than sitting telling stories to her grandchildren and making Victorian doll's houses with her husband.

Farbedrook

Farbedrook

Penelope Miller

ATHENA PRESS
LONDON

ISBN 10-digit: 1 84748 104 3
ISBN 13-digit: 978 1 84748 104 7

First published 2008 by
ATHENA PRESS
Queen's House, 2 Holly Road
Twickenham TW1 4EG
United Kingdom

Printed for Athena Press

For my children – Nikki, Bob and Fiona – and my grandchildren – Charlotte, Aimee, Josh, Toby, James, Hannah and baby Olivia

I would like to say a big thank you to my husband, Dusty, who took over the housework to allow me to write. I would also like to thank Scott, my next-door neighbour, for reading my rough copies and giving me his opinion.

Chapter One

There were once six children: Lottie, Lu-lu, Joshy-washy, Toby-two, Hanniepan and Jay-pee who lived with their mother, Mumsie Kinnie-winkie, in a faraway place called Farbedrook.

Every morning the children would see to the animals before going off to school. There was Plod the dog, Simon the cat, Jemima the chicken, Jack the duck, Buttercup the cow and Smarty-pants the horse. They had to get up very early each school day, and looked forward to school holidays when they could see to the animals and then have the rest of the day free to play and have adventures.

Farbedrook was a very nice place to live. Everybody was polite to each other, and the teachers only made you do the lessons that you liked best.

Everyone only ate the food that they loved best;

and as long as you didn't do anything bad, you could do what you wanted whenever you wanted

As it was so nice living in Farbedrook nobody ever left; though, strangely, nobody ever visited either.

It never rained in the summer in Farbedrook; in fact, they always had the best weather all the year. The winters had lovely snow to play in, and the only month that it rained was November.

In November it rained hard all month to fill up the water reservoirs.

Because of this, nobody went out in November. There was no school, and everyone just stayed at home and kept dry, but then on the last day of November it stopped raining and the sun shone, the school opened again and people came out of their homes. The sun shone until Christmas Eve, and then on that day, snow would begin to fall, and stay until the end of January. It was lovely snow: fluffy and white and it didn't make you cold and messy. All of Farbedrook's children loved to play out in it, having snowball fights and making snowmen. School always stayed closed until the first day in February to allow all the children to have fun in the snow.

In February, the spring flowers would bloom and the days would be pleasantly warm. The lovely warm weather would last right up to November when again the rains would come. The weather never differed, so you always knew exactly what it was going to be.

One summer day, when the schools were closed for the holidays, Mumsie Kinnie-winkie made a picnic for the children to take to Bedport Woods; this was one of their favourite places to go. They found a spot where there was some lovely trees to climb, and they put their picnic basket under one of them to keep cool in the shade.

They got out their ball and started to play a game called toof ball – they loved playing this. The ball was thrown and then you all chased it, jumping up so that you could catch the ball and bounce it off your nose. People with the biggest noses were the best players and Hanniepan with her enormous nose was constantly teased by the boys as they were secretly quite jealous of it. As usual, Lottie had to stop the boys from teasing her otherwise Hanniepan would start crying.

'Leave her alone!' she told them, sharply. The last thing they wanted on this lovely day was one of Hanniepan's famous tantrums.

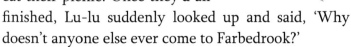

After playing a good game of toof ball, the children settled down under one of the trees to eat their picnic. Once they'd all finished, Lu-lu suddenly looked up and said, 'Why doesn't anyone else ever come to Farbedrook?'

'Don't be silly,' said Lottie, 'you know what Miss Fifoddy, our teacher, told us: we are the only people in this world. There are other people in another world, but they are very ugly, and thank goodness they can't get to us. I think that I would faint if I saw an ugly person, so I am very pleased they can't get to our world.'

'I don't believe that,' said Joshy-washy. 'I think that there are other people the other side of these woods, and I think that we should walk through and have a look.'

'Nooooo,' screamed Hanniepan, 'you know what Miss Fifoddy said. If we walk right through the woods, we will come to the end of the world, and then we will fall off, and goodness knows where we will end up. Maybe we will land on top of one of those ugly people she told us about.'

Toby-two and Jay-pee looked at each other. They thought it sounded like fun to see where the world ended, and maybe see one of these ugly people that everyone was always talking about. Toby-two had seen a book that had been hidden in the old wood-shed in the back garden, and he told the others about it.

'In the book, there were pictures of people with noses that were small, and eyes that were closer together than ours are, they also didn't have round faces. One of the girls was called Sleeping Beauty, and she was so ugly. She went to sleep for one hundred years until this man, who was just as ugly, came and kissed her, then she woke up. If you ask me it would have been far better if he had left her alone, so she could have stayed asleep for ever,' said Toby-two.

'Wow!' said Jay-pee. 'I would love to see that book, and I would also like to go through the woods to the end of the world to see if we can see some of these ugly people. Fancy being that ugly... She's even worse than Hanniepan!'

'Leave her alone!' warned Lottie.

Lottie said that she thought that they should all stop being silly, and if they were not going to play anymore games or climb any trees, they should all go home. Lu-lu and Hanniepan agreed, but the boys argued that they should at least walk to the end of the wood and just look over at the edge of the world to see what it looks like.

'Oh no,' said Lottie firmly. 'I am the eldest, and I am in charge, and we are all going to go home now, this very minute. Buttercup is waiting to be milked, and if we don't do it, nobody will have any milk for their cup of afternoon tea; and there will be no cake made for afters if we don't collect the eggs that Jemima has laid. Also, I shut Simon in the stable with

Smarty-pants this morning to catch the mice, and he will want to come out now – plus, Smarty-pants will be hungry for his hay. So if we were to fall off the edge of the world, who would do all these things?'

Plod the dog, who had been waiting for another game of toof ball to begin so that he could join in again, gave a half-hearted woof. He didn't want to go home yet, and looked at the boys and wagged his tail, hoping that they would refuse to go.

The boys looked at each other, and decided that they were not going to win against Lottie, who stood with her hands on her hips glaring at them.

'OK,' they said in unison, 'let's go then.' But they gave each other secret looks, and whispered that they would meet in the old wood shed later that evening to look at the book – without the girls.

Lottie, Lu-lu and Hanniepan milked the cow and collected the eggs, then made cakes for tea. The boys fed the horse and mucked out his stable, then walked down to the duck pond to feed the duck. All the time they were talking about the ugly people and the edge of the world.

'We have got to find out for ourselves,' they decided.

'Let's meet after dark in the woodshed,' said Joshy-washy.

'The book might give us some clues,' said Jay-pee.

'OK,' said Toby-two, 'I will bring my lantern. But don't say anything to the girls.'

After a lovely tea of sausage and mash which Mumsie Kinnie-winkie had cooked for them, the girls organised the boys to put the animals to bed; Plod wagged his tail knowingly at the boys.

'Shhhh!' whispered Jay-pee. 'If you keep looking at us like that, the girls will guess that there is something going on. If you get in your basket, when the girls are asleep I will come and get you.'

Plod did as he was told and got in his basket and laid down.

'Good boy,' said Jay-pee. 'See you soon.'

Ten o'clock came, and the boys crept out of their bedroom. All was quiet in the girls' room as they tiptoed by. Plod was waiting at the bottom of the stairs wagging his tail in anticipation.

The woodshed was very dark, but Toby-two had brought his lantern. The boys eased the door open and went inside and shut the door before lighting the lantern. Toby-two moved some old crates and reached behind them. There, hidden in an old cloth bag, was the book. Toby-two opened the bag and took it out; they all sat down on a big log and opened it. They shone the lantern on the pages and their mouths dropped open – on every page were pictures of the very ugly people.

'I wonder what world they live in,' said Joshy-washy.

'I bet it's the one at the end of our world, at the other side of the wood,' said Jay-pee.

'We have got to go and see,' said Toby-two.

'Let's go now,' said Jay-pee.

'No, we have to plan it carefully,' said Joshy-washy.

'We can't let the girls find out,' said Toby-two, 'you know how bossy Lottie and Lu-lu are. They will do anything to stop us going. We will start getting some things together and hide them somewhere safe. We will need ropes and pen knives.'

'And lots of food and drink,' added Jay-pee.

'Let's plan to go on Saturday,' said Joshy-washy. 'Then we'll have four days to plan and get everything together that we need.'

The other two agreed, and they started to read the book again.

'I think that we ought to take the book with us just in case we run into this girl called Sleeping Beauty or the prince, or any of these other ugly people that are in the book,' said Jay-pee.

'Good idea,' said Joshy-washy and Toby-two.

The boys hid the book back behind the old crates, they then blew the lantern out, and opened the shed door quietly; Plod started to run around all excited when they came outside. He thought that they were going on an adventure tonight, and he didn't fancy going back in the house just yet.

'We had better take him for a quick walk,' said Joshy-washy, 'else he is going to wake everyone up, and if the girls even get a little bit suspicious we will have to call it off.'

After taking Plod down the lane quickly, the boys quietly crept back into the house and back into their bedroom without disturbing the three girls.

The next few days were busy, with the boys trying to act normal while they collected all the things that they were likely to need for their trip to the edge of the world. They could hardly contain their excitement, and Plod was acting so silly that they decided that he could go with them.

'We might need him to protect us if we see any of those ugly people,' said Jay-pee.

'Good idea,' agreed the others.

The girls were surprised that the boys were doing all they asked them to do without any arguments. They didn't even tease Hanniepan,

'Something is not quite right,' said Lu-lu. 'They are never this nice to us, and they are always horrid to Hanniepan.'

'Just enjoy it while it lasts.' said Lottie.

Chapter Two

At last Saturday arrived, and after doing all the chores that the girls asked of them, the three boys and Plod met in the woodshed. They were all very excited. All of their lives they had heard about the edge of the world, but never did they dream that they would one day go to find it. They crept slowly and silently out of the woodshed and across the yard and out of the gate. Once out of the gate they ran, Plod by their side, down the lane and into Bedport Woods.

They followed the woodland paths until they came out of the other side of the woods, there at the end, was a line of trees, very close to one another and on one of the trees was an enormous notice. The boys ran up to it, so that they could read it; it said:

STOP!

DANGER!

DO NOT GO ANY FURTHER!

The boys were so engrossed reading the notice they didn't see a man come up behind them.

The man grabbed hold of Joshy-washy's shoulders, 'What do you think you are doing here?' he shouted at them.

The boys started to shake with fright. They knew they were going to be in big, big trouble.

'Who are you?' asked Toby-two.

'I am the keeper of the edge of the world, and my name is Mr Rebrotty,' he answered loudly.

'We only wanted to look.' spluttered Jay-pee.

'We want to go to another world,' said Toby-two, 'and see the very ugly people for ourselves.'

Joshy-washy joined in, saying that they had a book, and they wanted to go and look for the ugly person called Sleeping Beauty.

'Let me see this book,' said Mr Rebrotty.

The boys handed the book over and Mr Rebrotty studied the pages.

'I have heard that the people in the other world are ugly, but in a thousand years I didn't think that they were quite as ugly as this,' he shuddered. 'Right! I have thought about it, and I have decided that you can go and have a look over the edge. Mind you, you are only going to look, and it's on one condition: that I come with you,' said Mr Rebrotty.

The boys were disappointed. They wanted to go on their own, without any adults with them, but if this was the only way they could get to go, they would have to agree. 'OK,' they said in unison.

They all went through the trees, and stepped out onto the edge of a sheer drop. 'Wow!' the boys exclaimed. 'Look down there!'

'Don't go too near to the edge, in case you fall off,' said Mr Rebrotty. 'We don't know anything about the ugly people, they could very well be cannibals.'

'What are cannibals?' said Jay-pee.

'They are people who eat other people for their dinner,' said Joshy-washy.

'I don't want to be eaten,' said Jay-pee. 'In fact, it would be my worse nightmare!'

'Don't be daft,' said Joshy-washy. 'Who would want to eat you? I expect you would be very tough.'

Jay-pee lifted up his arm to hit out at Joshy-washy.

'Stop it, boys, stop arguing, I think that we should all go back now,' said Mr Rebrotty.

Toby-two got out the ropes. 'Actually, Mr Rebrotty, we have decided to climb down to the other world, just to have a quick peep.'

'I forbid it!' said Mr Rebrotty crossly.

Joshy-washy quickly tied the rope to the tree, and

was already half way down with Plod on his shoulders before Mr Rebrotty knew what was happening.

'Come back this minute!' shouted Mr Rebrotty.

Quick as a flash, Toby-two jumped on the rope as well, and started to slide down. Mr Rebrotty tried to grab him, but was too slow.

Jay-pee, not to be out done, jumped, and luckily managed to grab the rope, and he too began to slide down into the other world.

Mr Rebrotty was flabbergasted. He didn't know what to do. He was keeper of the edge of the world and his job was to stop anyone getting near to the edge. Not only had he let them near the edge, they had managed to slide down into the other world. He started to get very worried.

It was a very important job that he did, and if anyone found out that he had let the boys slide down into the other world, he would definitely lose his job. And if he lost his job, he would also lose his house, as the house, next to the line of trees, went with the job. The parish council that ruled their world would give his house and job to somebody else, then what would he do? He would have to go and live with either Old Man Disty-bun or Granny Nellie, and they would treat him like a slave. Instead of having the easy life he had now, he would have to peel potatoes and wash up all day.

Granny Nellie and Old Man Disty-bun cooked dinners for all the old people in Farbedrook, so he would be constantly working. 'I can't let this happen,' he said to himself. 'I will have to go after the boys and bring them back.'

Mr Rebrotty climbed gingerly onto the rope. He dared not look down; he didn't like heights. Slowly he let himself slide down and when he reached the bottom he quickly looked around. The boys were nowhere to be seen. He didn't dare call them in case someone from this other world heard him. He walked away from the rope and through a small wood. As he came to the other side he spotted the boys. They were looking at a strange-looking horse in a field. It didn't have an enormous nose and tiny eyes like their horses, and its legs were straight, not curly.

'What a funny-looking horse, boys,' he said.

The boys jumped and quickly turned around.

'Why have you followed us?' said Joshy-washy.

'I have come to keep an eye on you, and to make sure you don't get into any trouble,' Mr Rebrotty replied.

'Well, don't get in our way,' said Toby-two.

They all moved on. Plod was running ahead when suddenly he stopped and barked; the boys looked at one another and started to shake.

'Oh dear, I knew there would be trouble,' said Mr Rebrotty.

'Be quiet,' whispered Joshy-washy, 'somebody is coming.'

All of a sudden the most funny-looking, ugly little

girl came into view. 'Hello,' she called, 'if you don't mind me saying so, you are the funniest looking people I have ever seen.'

'Us! Funny looking!' said Toby-two. 'You are the ugliest person I have ever seen in my whole life. Look at you! Your nose is so small it looks silly. How on earth can you play toof ball?'

'What on earth is toof ball?' the girl said.

'Everybody knows what toof ball is,' said Jay-pee.

'Well, I don't,' replied the girl.

'You throw the ball up into the air, then you jump up and hit it with your nose, of course,' replied Jay-pee.

'I have never heard of anything so stupid in all my life,' said the girl. 'We play football here.'

'Football, what's that?' said Joshy-washy.

'You all chase the ball and kick it with your feet, then you kick it into a net, and that is called scoring a goal.'

'Sounds stupid to me,' said Jay-pee.

'Why are your eyes different and why isn't your head round?' said Toby two.

'I think you look really strange and odd,' added Joshy-washy.

'Well, I think that *you* all look odd,' said the girl. 'Where do you come from?'

Mr Rebrotty shouted, 'Don't tell her! She most probably wants to know so that she can tell everyone, and then they will all come into our world and eat us up.'

The girl started to laugh, and when she started she couldn't stop. She rolled around on the ground clutching her stomach as the laughter got louder and louder.

'Stop it! Stop it!' shouted Mr Rebrotty. 'Everyone will hear you.'

The girl stopped laughing, and with a smile on her face said, 'We don't eat people here. We eat sausages and mashed potatoes and chips and lots of other things, but not people.'

Mr Rebrotty felt a bit silly, and bent down to smooth Plod, to hide his red face.

'Shall we start again?' said the girl. 'My name is Jane. What are your names?'

The boys introduced them-selves, and explained that they came from a world that was called Farbedrook.

They all sat down under a tree, and the boys opened their bags and got out some of the food that they had brought. Jay-pee got the book of Sleeping Beauty and gave it to Jane, asking her if she knew where Sleeping Beauty lived. Jane started to laugh again.

'It's just a storybook,' she said. 'Everybody reads them when they are young. There are lots more; if you come again I will bring you some more to read. They are not real life.'

Jane started to ask them lots of things about their world, and was fascinated to hear about the weather and the fact that you only had to learn the lessons that you wanted to and you could eat whatever you wanted.

'Don't you have to eat cabbage and sprouts?' asked Jane.

'Never, YUK,' said Jay-pee.

'How wonderful, I wish I lived in your world,' said Jane. 'I would eat chocolate and ice cream all day long, and definitely no cabbage and sprouts.'

After about two hours of talking and comparing notes, Mr Rebrotty said that they ought to be making tracks for home. Jane walked with them back to the ropes, and the boys promised to come again the following Saturday.

'What an adventure,' said Jay-pee.

The others agreed. Mr Rebrotty made them all promise that they would keep quiet about it. He knew that if it ever came out that he had allowed the boys to go over the edge of the world he would definitely lose his job and home.

'I can't wait for next Saturday,' said Joshy-washy, and the others agreed.

They all started to climb the ropes, Mr Rebrotty stayed at the bottom until all the boys were safely back in Farbedrook, then he climbed up slowly. He wasn't as confident as the boys. He was a bit over-weight and it worried him that the rope wouldn't take his weight; it might break and send him plummeting back down again.

'Come on, Rotty,' the boys shouted.

'What did you call me?' Mr Rebrotty shouted.

'Rotty!' they shouted back.

Nobody had ever called him anything but Mr Rebrotty, but he quite liked it; it made him feel as though he was one of their friends. He couldn't remember having friends before. He didn't often see people, working as the keeper of the edge of the world, and it felt strangely good to be part of a group.

'Nearly there,' he shouted back, and then he was standing next to them, back in Farbedrook.

'In future, everyone can call me Rotty. I quite like it,' he said.

'OK, Rotty,' the boys said in unison.

'Can't wait for next Saturday,' said Jay-pee.

'I'm not sure that you should go down there again,' said Rotty.

'But we've got to! Jane will be waiting for us, and she is going to bring us some more books to read about ugly people, and I think that even though Jane is funny looking and very ugly, she is one of the nicest girls I have ever met,' said Joshy-washy.

'Well, she is not bossy like Lottie and Lu-lu or frightened of everything like Hanniepan,' said Toby-two.

The boys said goodbye to Rotty and started to make their way home through the woods. It was starting to get dark, and the woods seemed very spooky.

'Let's run,' said Jay-pee. The boys began to run.

'Come on, Plod,' Joshy-washy shouted.

'Where is he?' said Toby-two.

'You brought him up with you,' said Joshy-washy.

'No I didn't, I thought you brought him up,' replied Toby-two.

'You plonkers!' shouted Jay-pee. 'You have left him down in the other world.'

The boys stopped dead. 'Oh no! We have all forgotten him! What will he do by himself? Who will feed him?' said Joshy-washy.

'It's too dark now to go back and get him,' said Toby-two.

Jay-pee started to cry. 'Poor Plod, he will be so frightened by himself.'

'We will have to go back tomorrow,' said Joshy-washy. 'If we do our chores as quickly as we can in the morning, then we can hopefully sneak away without the girls spotting us.'

When they arrived home, Lottie was waiting, hands on hips. 'Where have you been until this time of day? It's dark outside and you know you are not allowed out after dark, without an adult with

you,' she shouted at them. 'Mumsy Kinnie-winkie is really cross with you all. She has gone to see Granny Nellie, but when she gets back you are all going to be in big trouble.'

'Sorry,' they all said, 'we were having such a good time climbing trees in Bedport Woods, we forgot the time.'

'Don't bother telling us,' said Lu-lu.

'It's Mumsy Kinnie-winkie you are going to have to explain yourselves to.'

'Where is Plod?' asked Hanniepan.

'Oh, he's out in the woodshed. He jumped in the stream and got a bit muddy, so he can't come indoors tonight. We have made him a nice bed out there,' lied Toby-two.

'I might go and see him in a minute to say good-night to him,' said Hanniepan.

'Nobody is going anywhere!' Lottie said firmly. The boys breathed a sigh of relief.

'I think we had better get ourselves ready for bed, before Mumsy Kinnie-winkie gets home,' said Joshy-washy.

'Good idea,' said Toby-two. 'Maybe, if Granny Nellie gives her some of her special apple and nettle wine, she might forget that we were in late.'

'Then let's get to bed as quickly as we can,' said Joshy-washy.

'I'm hungry,' whined Jay-pee.

'Forget about being hungry. We will be for it if we

are still up when Mumsy Kinnie-winkie gets in. We will be grounded for a week, then what will happen to Plod?' said Joshy-washy.

The next morning, the boys were up really early. Luckily Mumsy Kinnie-winkie had drunk rather a lot of Granny Nellie's apple and nettle wine, and she had forgotten about them coming home late. They rushed through all their chores, then met in the woodshed.

'Right then,' said Toby-two, 'we have got to get out quick before the girls ask where we are going.'

'We can't go just yet,' said Joshy-washy. 'Han-niepan is out in the yard playing with her skipping rope, and if she sees us going off somewhere she will want to come with us.'

'I know,' said Jay-pee, 'I will go out into the yard and ask her if she wants to play hide and seek. She loves playing that. If I let her hide first, as soon as she goes to find a hiding place, we can make a run for it.'

'Great idea,' said Joshy-washy and Toby-two.

Jay-pee ran out into the yard and over to Han-niepan. 'Do you want to play hide and seek?' he asked.

'Yes please,' she replied.

'OK, you can hide first,' said Jay-pee, and Han-niepan immediately ran off to hide.

As soon as she was out of sight, Jay-pee did a loud whistle and the other two boys came running out of the woodshed. Quick as lightning the boys ran across the yard and out the gate. They didn't stop running until they were in Bedport Woods and out of sight.

'Phew! That was close; I thought we were going to be seen. That was a brilliant idea of yours, Jay-pee,' said Joshy-washy.

'Right then, let's hurry now to the edge of the world,' said Toby-two, and the three boys started running again.

Chapter Three

When the boys arrived at the row of trees in front of the edge of the world, they expected Rotty to be there, and were most surprised when he wasn't. They ran past and got to the edge.

'Thank goodness our ropes are still here tied to the trees,' said Toby-two. He quickly jumped on and started to slide down; the other two followed him.

When they got to the bottom, they started to whistle and call for Plod.

'He must be around here somewhere,' said Jay-pee.

'Let's go to where we met Jane yesterday and see if he's there,' said Joshy-washy.

The boys made their way there, and looked around. They called and whistled, but still there was no sign of Plod.

'There is a funny-looking house up there,' said Joshy-washy. 'Let's go up and see if he's there.'

The boys walked up to the funny square house. 'I wonder who would live in a house like this,' said Jay-pee. 'Everyone knows all houses are round. It's all very odd in this world.'

The front door of the house opened and Jane came running out.

'I am so glad you have come back,' she said. 'You forgot to take your dog with you yesterday, and after you left, the dog warden came along and caught hold of him and put him in his van. I tried to stop him, but he knew he wasn't my dog. He said because he didn't have a collar on, he had to take him to the dogs' home.'

'What's a dogs' home?' said Joshy-washy.

'It's a place for stray animals. They live there until somebody claims them, or someone else offers them a home. But the warden said that Plod was so funny looking nobody would want him. So, after fourteen days he would be put to sleep,' said Jane.

'I hate that warden saying Plod was funny looking. He is the best-looking dog ever, and why would Plod want to go to sleep?' said Jay-pee.

'He wouldn't want to go to sleep; the warden would put him to sleep. Don't you know what that means?' said Jane. The boys all shook their heads. 'It means he would be dead,' Jane added.

'Dead! What do you mean dead? Are you saying that the warden would kill him? Why on earth would anyone want to kill Plod? He is the best dog in the world,' cried Jay-pee.

'What are dog wardens anyway?' said Toby-two. 'We don't have them in Farbedrook.'

Jane looked at him in astonishment. 'You don't

have dog wardens? Who collects all the stray animals then?'

'We don't have any stray animals. Our animals just walk around wherever they want. There are no rules like that.'

'I would really like to see your world,' said Jane wistfully. 'It sounds fun.'

'Can we stick to the point? Plod is trapped and we need to get him back.' said Joshy-washy.

The others agreed, so they all sat down on the grass to make plans.

'Why don't we all just go to the dogs' home and ask for him back?' said Jay-pee.

'It doesn't work that way,' said Jane. 'Firstly you will have to prove that he is your dog, then if they agree, you will have to pay the fine.'

'What's a fine?' asked Toby-two.

'It's the amount of money that you have to give to them, for letting your dog stray on his own.'

'I have got half a crown in my pocket,' said Joshy-washy.

This time it was Jane who was puzzled. 'What on earth is half a crown,' she asked.

'Two and sixpence,' said Jay-pee.

Jane still looked puzzled and said, 'I think that it will be around fifty pounds.'

'Fifty pounds!' the boys said in unison. 'That's a fortune! You can nearly buy a house for that amount.

'Don't be silly,' she replied. 'If I am good I get forty pounds a month pocket money, and it's certainly not that much money.'

'Well, we certainly don't have that sort of money,' the boys replied.

'We are lucky if we get a sixpenny piece a week pocket money.'

'I think that you must have different money in your world,' said Jane. 'We have six pence, but not a sixpenny piece. Wait here a minute and I will go inside to get my money box. I have got some money saved in it from my pocket money over the last few months. I was saving up to buy a bicycle, but I can make do with my old one for a bit longer,' said Jane.

Jane ran back to the funny square house and went inside.

'What's a bicycle?' asked Jay-pee.

'I have not got the faintest idea,' said Joshy-washy, 'but I expect we will find out.'

After a few minutes, Jane came running out. 'QuÍck,' she shouted, 'Run before Mummy looks out of the window. If she sees me she will call me back.'

The four of them took off at a fast pace.

'Where are we going?' panted Jay-pee.

'To the dogs' home,' replied Jane.

After about ten minutes they arrived at a large square building, and Jane stopped outside.

'This is it,' she said, 'Bloomsbury Dogs' Home.'

The large blue doors to the building were tightly closed, and the four children gingerly went up to them and knocked gently; nobody answered.

'I think we have to knock a bit harder,' said Jane, and proceeded to give the door a very hard bang. Within a couple of minutes the door creaked open, and a very tall man looked down at them.

'That's him, the dog warden,' whispered Jane.

'Do you kids think it's Halloween?' shouted the man crossly. 'Go and take those grotesque masks off, and don't bother me again.'

'We haven't got masks on,' protested a very offended Joshy-washy.

'Mr Dog Warden,' began Jane very politely, 'these are my new friends and they come from another world called Farbedrook, and they can't help looking like this. Everyone in their world looks the same as them, and they think that we look extremely ugly and funny. They are very nice people and they have come to claim their dog, who you picked up yesterday and brought here.'

'What dog?' replied the dog warden.

'You remember, I spoke to you when you caught him, and I told you he wasn't a stray, and that he belonged to my friends, but you wouldn't believe me.'

'Oh, I remember now,' the man said. 'The ugly, funny-looking one. The one I said that nobody would want. The one with the curly legs, a big nose and funny eyes. Come to think of it, he looks a bit like you funny kids.'

This was just too much for Jay-pee, somebody criticising his beloved Plod, and he flew at the man with fists flying. The children just managed to catch hold of him before he got to the man.

'No!' they shouted at him. 'That's not the way.'

'No, it certainly is not,' the warden said. 'If you had hit me, I would have to call the police, and then you definitely would not have got your ugly dog back.'

'Calm down, everyone,' said Jane. 'Can we please just see their dog, Mr Warden?'

'You had better come in then, but if there is one little bit of trouble I will throw you out and call the police.'

The boys didn't know who 'the police' were, but they didn't sound very nice. Thank goodness they didn't have them in their world.

The man opened the doors wide to let the children in. They followed him down a passage way until they came to a long room with a padlock on the door. The warden got out his keys and opened it up. Inside the room were loads of cages; each one had a dog inside it. As soon as they went inside, all the dogs started to bark. The man walked along past all the cages, until he came to the one at the very end.

Inside the last cage lay Plod. He didn't bark, rather he just lay there feeling sorry for himself but when he saw the boys he got up and ran to the cage door, wagging his twisty tail.

'Well, he seems to know you,' said the warden. 'He hasn't moved since I put him in there yesterday, and he wouldn't eat his dog food last night or this morning.'

'He only eats sausages, burgers and ice cream,' said Jay-pee.

'Sausages and ice cream!' said the warden. 'Nobody feeds their dogs sausages and ice cream.'

'In our world, everyone eats whatever they want to eat,' said Jay-pee.

'Well your world must be an extremely silly world then,' said the warden. He opened the cage and let a jubilant Plod out. 'This is going to cost you a thirty-five-pound fine, and you are lucky that I am feeling generous today, or else it would have cost you fifty pounds.'

The children followed the warden back past all the other cages full of barking dogs, out through the door and back to a little office. He went to a desk and pulled out a form, which he filled in and gave to them.

'You owe me thirty-seven pounds and fifty pence.'

'You said just now that it was thirty-five pounds,' said Toby-two.

'What is the extra two pounds fifty for?' said Jane.

'A collar and lead,' said the warden, 'because if you take him out of here without a collar and lead on, I will have to fine you again.'

He reached into his desk drawer and pulled out a red collar and lead, and gave it to the boys to put on Plod. Plod had never had a collar and lead on before, and crouched down fearfully when Toby-two put it on him.

'This is the strangest thing; it looks a bit like Old Man Disty-bun's belt that he always wears. How on earth do I put it on poor Plod?' said Toby-two.

'It's quite easy,' said Jane and she knelt down beside Toby-two to show him how it fitted.

'The collar must not be too tight,' she said as she quickly put the collar round Plod's neck and fastened it. Giving the end of the lead to Toby-two, she told him that he must keep hold of the end of the lead until they got home.

'Don't worry, boy. You won't have to wear it when we get back to Farbedrook,' said Jay-pee. 'Just while we are in this funny place.'

Jane got out her purse, and paid the warden the thirty-seven pounds and fifty pence, and they all made a hasty retreat out the door.

'How are we ever going to repay you?' asked Josh-washy.

'Don't worry about it for now,' said Jane. 'Let's get back to the ropes so that you can get Plod back to Farbedrook.'

'One thing I would like to ask you, Jane,' said Toby-two, 'what on earth is a bicycle?'

'Don't you have bicycles in your world?' asked Jane. The boys all shook their heads. 'When we get back to my house, I will run in and get my old bicycle out, so that you can see it. And I will get those books I promised to lend you too.'

Jane's house came in to view and, while she ran inside, the boys sat down on the grass. Plod rolled on his back to have his tummy tickled.

'Thank goodness we found you,' said Jay-pee.

Plod gave each of the boys a big sloppy lick. He was very glad that they had found him as well.

Chapter Four

Jane came out of her garden gate pushing the funniest thing the boys had ever seen. It had two wheels, and two strange things sticking out the sides, and a thing that looked a bit like a seat on it.

'Is that a bicycle?' asked Joshy-washy. 'Whatever do you do with it?'

'You ride it,' said Jane.

At this the boys began to laugh. 'We ride horses in Farbedrook, not funny things like that,' they said.

'We ride horses as well sometimes, but a bicycle is fun, and you don't have to feed it or brush it!' Jane got on the bicycle, and started to pedal it down the lane. The boys laughed but thought it looked good fun, and couldn't wait to have a go on it.

Joshy-washy, being the biggest, had first go. He sat

on the funny seat, put his feet on the funny things that stuck out the side, which Jane called pedals, and promptly fell off.

Jane laughed. 'You have to get your balance first, before you put both feet on the pedals,' she said.

Joshy-washy tried a few more times; then he took off and managed to go a few metres before falling off. 'You have a go,' he said to Toby-two.

Toby-two was a bit reluctant when he saw Joshy-washy's scraped knee from falling off.

'Go on,' said Joshy-washy, 'I have tried, so now it's your turn.'

Toby-two got on the bike, and after falling off a few times managed, like Joshy-washy, to stay on for a few metres. Jay-pee wanted to try and, like the other two, managed to keep from falling off for a short way after a few tries.

The boys all said that they would love to have a bicycle of their own, and Jane promised them that when she had a new bicycle she would give them her old one for them all to share.

They arrived back to the edge of the world and walked over to where the ropes were.

'Oh no,' cried Joshy-washy, 'the ropes have disappeared.'

'They can't have,' said the others. 'Who would have taken them?'

Jay-pee started to cry. 'Now we will never get back home, we will have to stay here for ever, and eat sprouts and cabbage every day, and Plod will always have to have this horrid collar and lead on. And we will never see the girls and Mumsy Kinnie-winkie ever again.' He collapsed down on the ground and started to cry very loudly.

Jane sat down next to him. 'Don't worry, Jay-pee, we will find a way for you to go home.' She put her arms round him and gave him a big cuddle.

'Pull yourself together, Jay-pee,' said Toby-two. 'Crying doesn't solve anything.'

Jay-pee sat up, and Jane took a large handkerchief out of her pocket, and wiped the tears from his funny round face.

'I have got an idea,' said Jane. 'Stay here, while I go and see my friend Harry. He will know what to do, he is really intelligent.'

Jane ran off, and the other two boys sat down on the grass next to Jay-pee. Plod snuggled close to them. He knew that something wasn't quite right, and he gave them all a big lick on their hands.

'It's going to be OK, Plod, don't worry,' Joshy-washy said, but deep down, Joshy-washy was very worried. He couldn't let the other two see that he was anxious, because, being the eldest of the three, he felt that it was his responsibility to keep them safe.

It seemed ages before Jane was back, but all of a sudden she was there, with this boy called Harry. Harry stared at them, and they stared back, each of them thinking the other was really funny looking.

Jane introduced them all, and told them that Harry was going to borrow the woodman's ladder.

'He has got a very long ladder,' said Harry, 'so hopefully it will reach back into your world.' Harry ran off to get the ladder.

'I told you that Harry would be able to help you, didn't I?' said Jane.

They all sat down again on the grass to wait for Harry's return. 'What if the ladder isn't long enough?' asked Jay-pee.

'If it's not, then Harry will think of something else,' said Jane.

After about half an hour, Harry returned with the woodman's ladder. He put it up the side of the edge of the world, and pushed up the extension parts.

'It's not long enough,' he said. 'Try climbing up the ladder as far as you can, then see if there is anything that you can catch hold of to climb up the rest of the way.'

'I will do it, as I am the biggest,' said Joshy-washy, and proceeded to climb the ladder to the top.

'It's no good,' he shouted down from the top, 'there is nothing to catch hold of, but I can see the ropes from here. Somebody has pulled them up and wound them in a coil at the top of the edge of the

world. I'm coming down now.' He quickly slid down the ladder.

When he got to the bottom, he told them all how the ropes had obviously been pulled up by someone, then coiled around very neatly.

'I wonder who did that?' said Toby-two.

'It must have been Rotty,' said Joshy-washy. 'We didn't see him before we came down today. He most probably pulled them up so that nobody could climb up them from this world down here; you know how he thinks that most people from this world would like to eat people from Farbedrook. What are we going to do?'

It was starting to get dark.

'Where are we going to sleep?' said Jay-pee.

'I'm thinking,' said Joshy-washy.

'I don't think that my mummy will let you all sleep in my house,' said Jane.

'I know,' said Harry, 'you can all sleep in my stables. My pony is sleeping out in the field at the moment, and there is lots of hay to keep you all warm. I will smuggle you out some supper to eat, and then we will think of a plan in the morning.'

The boys followed him and Jane to his stables. They went inside and sat down on some hay bales.

Jane said that she had better go home, but that she would see them all in the morning, Harry said that he had better go too, but that he would make an excuse to come out again after supper. He would bring them all out something to eat.

When he closed the door to the stable it was very dark.

'I'm a bit scared,' said Jay-pee.

'I have got my lantern in my rucksack,' said Toby-two, 'but we must not keep it lit all the time, as the candle is getting low.'

'I hope Harry doesn't bring us out cabbage and sprouts to eat,' said Jay-pee.

'Anything is better than nothing,' said Toby-two.

Joshy-washy just said, 'YUK!'

About an hour later, the boys heard someone running across the yard.

'Quick, blow out the lantern,' hissed Joshy-washy.

Toby-two turned it off. The door opened and somebody quickly came in. 'Where are you all?' whispered Harry.

The boys breathed a sigh of relief and lit the lantern again, 'Why were you all sitting in the dark, when you have a lantern?' said Harry.

'We blew it out, in case it wasn't you coming,' said Joshy-washy.

'Good thinking,' said Harry.

On his back, Harry had a rucksack. He took it off and opened it up. Inside were cheese sandwiches, ham sandwiches, slices of fruit cake and jam tarts. To wash it all down there were two large bottles of lemonade.

'WOW!' said the boys. 'We thought that you might bring us cabbage and sprouts.

'No, I hate cabbage and sprouts, and my mum doesn't make me eat them,' said Harry.

'How did you get all this food out, without anyone seeing you?' said Joshy-washy.

'Easy,' said Harry, 'Mum and Dad were going to the cinema tonight, so after supper I was on my own. Hurry up and eat, then you can come into my house and see my toys and things.'

The boys didn't have the faintest idea what a cinema was, but decided to keep quiet about it.

The boys quickly ate all the food, then followed Harry across the yard and into the strange square house. Inside the kitchen, there was all sorts of odd things, Harry showed them the microwave, fridge, washing machine, dish washer, and was amazed that they didn't have things like that in their world. Then he took them into the lounge and put the television on. The boys jumped back in terror as an enormous dinosaur leapt out and attacked some people. Jay-pee started to run out of the room.

'It's not real,' said Harry, 'it's just a film.' Harry started to laugh. 'Are you going to tell me that you don't have television in your world, either?' The boys shook their heads; they still looked as if they were going to run for their lives, away from the dinosaur.

'How did that animal and people get in that box?' asked Jay-pee.

'They are not really in there, it's just a film,' said Harry. 'Don't be scared,' he laughed, 'they can't get out.'

Harry took them upstairs to his bedroom. On the floor running all round the room was a train track, with a model train on.

'Wow!' said Joshy-washy. 'We do have trains in our world, but our trains always have lots of smoke coming out of their funnels and I have never seen one this small. It's too small for people to ride on, unless you have some very tiny people living in your world.'

'No, silly, it's a toy train, same as all these other toys.' Harry opened the doors to the toy cabinet to show them all his toys. The boys were gob-smacked; they had never seen anything like it. Harry took lots of things out, and showed them how they worked. All the boys could keep saying was 'Wow!'

'What kind of toys do you have?' Harry asked them.

'We have books, and some toy animals, and the girls have dolls and skipping ropes, and we all have balls. Toof ball is the favourite game in our world.'

'Jane told me about that when she came to get me today. That is obviously why you have rather large noses,' said Harry.

'Well, I think that your noses are silly and small,' said Jay-pee defensively.

'That is why you kick the ball and call it football,' said Toby-two, 'because your noses are too small.'

'I wish we had toys like these,' said Jay-pee. 'Look at this one: it's got wheels so that you can push it along, but it's not a wheel barrow. It's got seats inside.'

'It's a car!' said Harry. 'Don't you have cars either?' Harry jumped up. 'Come with me,' he said, and the boys all followed him. Harry went outside the house, took them around the back, to where a large shed was.

'Are we going into this shed?' said Toby-two.

'It's not a shed, it's a garage,' said Harry.

'A what?' said the boys.

'Never mind, just come inside,' Harry said, and the boys followed him. In this place called a garage was a big car, the same as the toy one that Harry had just shown them. Harry opened the car doors and invited them to sit inside.

'What does it do?' the boys asked.

'You drive it.'

'What! The same as we drive Smarty-pants, our horse, when he pulls the cart along?'

'No, you start up the engine; it doesn't need a horse to pull it. Look, I will show you.' Harry turned the key in the car's ignition and the car immediately sprung into life. The boys had never heard engine noises before and were fascinated.

'What happens now?' asked the boys.

Harry put the car into drive, took the handbrake off, and the car slowly began to move out of the garage. The boys' mouths dropped open; none of them dared speak. Harry knew that really he wasn't allowed to drive the car, but he was enjoying showing off, and couldn't resist driving it round and round his driveway before manoeuvring it back into the garage again.

'That was fantastic,' the boys all said. 'Wish we had cars in Farbedrook.'

After they had got out of the car, Harry took them back up into his bedroom, and they all played for ages with the toy cars. All of a sudden Harry looked at his watch. 'You had better go back into the stable soon, because Mum and Dad will be home at ten, and it's a quarter to ten now.

The boys made their way back downstairs, out into the yard and back into the stable. 'See you all in the morning,' said Harry. 'I will bring you something for breakfast.' Then he was gone.

The boys couldn't sleep, their heads were all full of all the strange things they had seen: machines to wash and dry clothes, machines to wash and dry dishes. What Mumsy Kinnie-winkie would do for one of those machines. Cupboards that were so cold there was ice in them all the time. Harry called it a refrigerator. Then a thing called a microwave oven that heated up things and cooked your dinner in minutes. Water that you didn't have to fetch from the well, you just turned on a tap and out it came; hot water without having to boil it up, you just turned on another tap. Then that large thing that looked as though there was people stuck in it called a television. But the best thing of all was that large car that they had sat in, and that Harry had driven round and round the driveway. What an adventure! If they managed to get back into their world, what stories they would have to tell to all the children at school. The girls would be green with envy!

Thinking about the girls suddenly brought them back to reality. Mumsy Kinnie-winkie, Lottie, Lu-lu and Hanniepan would all be worried about them. They would be thinking that the monster of the lake had got them. They had been learning about the monster of the lake in school, and all the children said that they would never go near the lake again.

'I bet they are all out searching for us,' said Toby-two. 'Mumsie Kinnie-winkie would have rushed around to Granny Nellie's and Old Man Disty-bun's, and they would have called other people to go with them to search for us.'

'There is nothing we can do about it, as we are stuck here. Harry has said that he has a brilliant idea that he is going to see about tomorrow. All we can do is wait until then,' said Joshy-washy.

'Let's all try and get some sleep, or else we are going to be too tired to do anything tomorrow,' said Toby-two. So the boys all lay down in the soft hay. Although they all said that they would not be able to get to sleep, it wasn't long before all you could hear in the stable was the three boys and Plod snoring softly, as they dreamt of the adventures that they had had that day.

Chapter Five

The boys were woken up by a rattling as the stable door was opened. 'It's OK, it's only me,' called Harry. 'Mum and Dad have both gone to work, and won't be back until this evening, so you can come into the house and have something to eat for breakfast.'

The boys eagerly followed Harry across the yard and into the house.

'I have had the most marvellous idea,' said Harry. 'The problem you have got is that there is no way that you can climb back up to your world because it is too steep, and there isn't a ladder long enough to reach the top. Well, I hardly slept all night, thinking about all of this, and I suddenly thought of Mr Jones.'

'Who is Mr Jones, and what's he got to do with anything?' said Jay-pee.

'Be quiet and listen to what Harry has to say,' said Joshy-washy.

Harry continued, 'Mr Jones is a hot air balloonist. If I can get him to agree, he could fly his hot air

balloon back up to your world and deliver you back home.'

The boys sat there with confused faces. They had no idea what on earth a hot air balloon was and wondered when they should tell Harry that only birds could fly. But they kept quiet, knowing that in this world everything was different.

'I will go and see Mr Jones straight after breakfast. Now, does everyone want toast?' said Harry.

The boys looked around for a fire to do the toast on, but looked on in amazement when Harry put slices of bread in a funny-looking silver box with slots in the top. Within a couple of minutes, the bread had popped up again and it had magically turned into toast.

'Wow!' was all the boys could say.

After breakfast, Harry took off to go and see Mr Jones. Before he left he told the boys that they could go up and play with the toys in his bedroom if they wanted to. Did they want to? Did they ever! They couldn't wait to get up there to play with all of Harry's fantastic toys. The time went so quickly, and before long the whole morning had gone.

'Harry has been a rather long time,' said Joshy-washy.

'I don't care how long he is,' said Jay-pee, 'I just love playing with all his toys! I don't want to go home yet.'

Just as Jay-pee said that, the boys heard the front door open and Harry's voice shout to them to come downstairs and meet Mr Jones.

The boys ran downstairs and found themselves facing quite a short man, with a large bushy moustache that curled up at each end. The boys had never seen such a big moustache.

'Harry was right when he said that you were all rather odd-looking,' said Mr Jones.

'Well, we don't think that we are odd looking. We think that you are all odd and ugly-looking,' said Jay-pee.

Joshy-washy kicked him in the shins. 'Shut up!' he whispered. 'If you are rude, he might not help us.'

'Right,' said Mr Jones, 'hopefully, if the weather is right, we will be able to get the hot air balloon off the ground tomorrow. I will get it all ready and when I am ready for you I will telephone Harry to bring you to Farmer Ted's field, then if all is well, you can all get in the basket and we can take off and get you home.'

It was all too confusing for the boys, talk of telephones, getting in baskets and flying was all alien to them.

'Thank you very much,' Joshy-washy managed to say.

'I'm glad that we are not going until tomorrow. Now we get to play with the toys longer,' said Jay-pee, with a great big smile on his face.

Mr Jones left then, as he said that he had lots of arranging to do if they wanted to fly tomorrow.

'Does this basket thing that we are going to fly in have wings?' asked Toby-two.

'No,' laughed Harry, 'it's a great big balloon powered by gas, which is lit so that the flames from the gas keep the balloon up in the sky. The basket that carries everyone is tied to the balloon, so that it flies through the air or something like that. I'm not really up on hot air ballooning, but I think that's right. Mr Jones will tell us all about it in the morning. I'm really excited as well, because Mr Jones said that I can come along with you all for the ride.'

'Have you ever been in one of these balloons before?' said Joshy-washy.

'No, never. I have watched Mr Jones going up in the air and landing again in his loads of times, and I have always wondered what it would be like to go up in it,' said Harry.

'Can you take us for a ride in the big car again?' said Jay-pee.

'No, I daren't. I shouldn't have really taken you yesterday; my parents would have grounded me for a month if they knew. You have to be seventeen years old and have a driving licence before you are allowed to drive. And even then you have to pass a driving test first. I didn't really break the law, because I only drove the car around the drive, not out on the road, but if my parents found out... I would have been in big trouble,' said Harry.

All of a sudden, there was a loud noise coming from the sky, the boys looked out of the window to see a strange-looking thing whirling around.

'What on earth is that!' said Toby-two.

'It's a helicopter. The blades going around on the top of it makes it fly, I think. I don't know much about helicopters, I have never been on one. But I do go on an aeroplane every year, when we go on our holidays. I'll bet you don't know what they are either, do you? If we go back upstairs I will show you. I have got toy aeroplanes and helicopters.'

The boys all went back upstairs, and Harry showed them all his toy planes; they were fascinated.

'When we get home, nobody is going to believe us about all these things,' said Joshy-washy.

'Oh no!' Harry suddenly said.

'What's up?' said the boys.

'I have just been thinking that when I go on holiday, I fly right up in the sky. Why don't I or anybody else ever see your world, and why doesn't the helicopter, which is always flying around, see your world?'

'I don't know,' said Toby-two. 'I think that the

only way back up to your world must be where you climbed down, and that must be in some kind of time warp.'

'What does that mean then?' said Joshy-washy.

'It means that, no matter how high Mr Jones flies his hot air balloon, there is no way he is going to get to your world. The only way up is to take you up the way you came down.'

'I am going to have to telephone Mr Jones and tell him, before he makes arrangements with Farmer Ted to take off from his field.'

Harry rushed downstairs to make the call. The boys came out of the bedroom and peered over the banisters to watch Harry pick up this thing that you put to your ear one end and spoke in the other end. By now they had stopped being surprised by the odd things in this world.

Harry soon explained to Mr Jones that they wouldn't be able to take off from Farmer Ted's field. When he had finished talking, Harry went back upstairs and told the boys about the change in plans.

'Right, Mr Jones is going to try to take off at the bottom of the edge that you came down. He can't promise that it will work, but he is willing to give it a try. We must not tell anyone, because they might try to stop him, as taking off there could be quite hazardous. OK?'

'OK!' they all replied excitedly.

'I am going to fix you all some dinner now, because

it's only a couple of hours before Mum and Dad will be starting off to get home from work.'

Harry and Joshy-washy went downstairs to the kitchen. Jay-pee and Toby-two stayed in Harry's room playing with all the cars and aeroplanes.

'I wish that we had things like this in our world,' said Jay-pee.

'I agree,' said Toby-two, 'life is going to seem really boring when we get back to Farbedrook.'

Down in the kitchen, Harry was explaining how all the gadgets in the house worked. Joshy-washy was intrigued by everything.

'I wonder if we will ever have gadgets like these in our world,' he said.

'Do you think that you will ever come down here again?' asked Harry.

'I really hope so,' said Joshy-washy. 'I really like you and Jane; I would hate it if we never saw you again.'

'Well, you have got to come again, because Jane is giving you her old bike when she gets a new one.'

'I had forgotten about that,' said Joshy-washy.

'I know!' said Harry as a wonderful idea came to him. 'Jane and I could come up to your world. I would love to see it. You could let down the ropes for us to climb up, then hide them so nobody could take them, and get them out again when it's time to slide down.'

'What a good idea, Harry! I would love you to meet the girls. Lottie is the eldest, then Lu-lu – they are both a bit bossy – then there's Hanniepan; she is a

bit shy, and sometimes she cries a bit, but she is
lovely. She is Jay-pee's twin, you know.'

'I didn't know Jay-pee was one of a twin,' said Harry.
'Do they look the same?'

'Not much. They have got different colour hair,
and Hanniepan's nose is bigger. Jay-pee is a bit jealous
of that.'

'Why? I can't think of any reason that somebody
would be jealous of a big nose. In this world, if you
have a big nose, people will make fun of you,' said
Harry.

'Not in our world,' said Joshy-washy. 'It's a sign of
beauty, and the bigger nose you have the better you can
play toof ball. Everyone wants to play the best toof ball.'

'I can't wait to see your world,' said Harry. 'I hope
that we can come before the summer holidays end.'

Harry called the others down to eat
their dinner, 'I have done beef burgers
and chips, followed by ice cream, and
there is a bowl with beef burger and
ice cream in for Plod too,' said
Harry.

'Oh scrummy!' said the boys.

'I have been wondering,' said Harry, 'if you don't have refrigerators and freezers in your world, how do you have ice cream?'

'That's easy, silly,' said Jay-pee.

'Don't be so rude, Jay-pee, it's not nice to keep calling people silly.' scolded Toby-two. 'I will tell you, Harry,' said Toby-two. 'There is a big pit called the ice pit, and every few days we go there to get ice, then we bring it home on the wheel barrow. Mumsy Kinnie-winkie puts it a barrel and then she makes the ice cream, and puts it in the barrel to freeze.'

'I bet your Mumsy Kinnie-winkie would like a refrigerator and freezer like ours,' said Harry.

After eating their dinner, Harry gave the boys a packet of biscuits and some crisps and lemonade to take out in the stable with them, in case they got hungry or thirsty before morning.

'I will try to come out and see you this evening before I go to bed,' said Harry, 'but I can't promise anything.'

'What would happen if your Mum or Dad saw us?' asked Toby-two.

'They wouldn't be nasty or anything,' said Harry, 'but they would want to know why you were here without an adult, and most probably they would get in touch with somebody, to keep you safe. Then you could be taken away so that the authorities could find out more about you, and then it could be months before you got back to your world. The thing is most of the adults wouldn't believe anything about your world, because it is so different to ours. There are a few people that do believe that there are other worlds out there. Mr Jones is one of them, so we know that we can trust him, but I think it is best that you just keep yourself hidden until we are ready to go.'

'When you come up into our world it will be the same,' said Joshy-washy. 'You look so different; we will have to find a good place to hide you up there. When we get back, we will start making the old wood shed into a good place to stay.'

'I am really looking forward to coming,' said Harry.

The boys went out the door and across the yard to the stable, and settled themselves in on the hay.

'I have had such a wonderful day today,' said Jay-pee, the other two agreed that it was the best day ever. They couldn't stop talking about all the things that they had seen and found out about.

When it was dark, Joshy-washy said that he didn't think that Harry was coming out to see them, and after organising a snack of the biscuits and crisps and a drink of lemonade, he said that they ought to try and get some sleep, so that they had loads of energy the next day.

'I don't think that I will ever be able to get to sleep tonight, after all the exciting things I have seen today,' said Jay-pee.

The other two agreed, but within ten minutes all three of them were fast asleep.

Chapter Six

The next morning the boys were awake bright and early, waiting for Harry to come and get them.

At just after nine, Harry ran into the stable. 'Come on,' he shouted, 'Mum and Dad have left for work and breakfast is ready. I bet you are quite hungry. I have made bacon, sausages and scrambled eggs, and we can wash it down with mugs of hot chocolate.'

'Cor, that sounds lovely,' the boys all said, and they hurried out of the stable, across the yard and into the warm kitchen of the house.

'That smells so good,' said Joshy-washy, and they all sat at the table and devoured it all, finishing up with toast and marmalade.

'If I ate another thing I would burst,' said Jay-pee.

'Thank you very much, Harry' said the boys, wiping their mouths.

After loading all their dirty plates and things in the dishwasher, they all got ready to go and meet Mr Jones.

'Let's go over to Jane's first, because I am sure that she would want to come and see you off,' said Harry.

The four boys started out down the lane to Jane's house. Jane was pleased that they had called for her and she quickly got herself ready to come with them.

As they walked along they were comparing notes from their two worlds.

'I can't wait to come and see your world,' said Jane. 'Harry's really lucky to be coming with you and Mr Jones today. I wish there was room for me.'

'What will we do if Mr Jones's hot air balloon will not go up into our world? asked Jay-pee. 'That would mean I would never see Mumsy Kinnie-winkie, the girls and Granny Nellie ever again.' Jay-pee's eyes welled up and great big tears started to run down his funny, round face.

Jane put her arms round him and gave him a big hug. 'Don't cry Jay-pee,' she said. 'Mr Jones will find a way to take you home.'

Jay-pee stopped crying and Jane wiped his eyes with her clean handkerchief.

'Right, everyone,' said Harry, 'let's get a move on. Mr Jones will be there by now and we don't want him thinking we are not going to turn up. He might just pack up his things and go home!'

The children ran through the lanes and up into the small wooded area that sat at the bottom of the edge of the boys' world.

Mr Jones had already set up his hot air balloon. 'I

was beginning to think that you were not coming,' he said to them.

'Sorry,' they all puffed, 'we are just running a bit late.'

When Joshy-washy, Toby-two and Jay-pee saw the hot air balloon, they couldn't believe their eyes. They had never seen anything like it in their lives. The basket that they were going to get into had big sacks of something inside.

Mr Jones told them that they hung the bags on the outside for ballast. The boys hadn't the slightest idea what he meant, but it all looked very impressive. They ran to the edge and peered inside. They couldn't wait to get in – to actually fly!

'Are you ready then?' said Mr Jones.

The boys all gave Jane a quick hug, then climbed inside the basket, making sure that they put Plod in first, so that he was not left behind again.

'See you soon,' Jane said, 'and don't forget I am coming up into your world for a visit. I will bring my old bicycle for you all, because Dad and Mum said that they are going to buy me a new one for my birthday next month.'

There was an almighty roar as the flames leapt up, and the balloon seemed to expand. The next moment they had left the ground.

'We're flying, really flying!' shouted Jay-pee excitedly. 'Just like a bird!'

The boys looked down and saw Jane waving and shouting.

'Good luck, see you again very soon,' they shouted back.

The balloon went higher and higher, right up the edge of the cliff, where the boys had climbed down on the rope. It wasn't long before they could see their world again.

'We are here, we're back!' shouted Toby-two.

'Look, there is Rotty's house.'

'Who is Rotty?' said Harry.

'He is the keeper of the edge of the world,' said Joshy-washy.

'Look!' said Toby-two. 'Rotty has heard us, and has come out of his house to see what the noise is.'

The children started to shout and wave at him.

'Rotty, Rotty, it's us! Look, we are flying!' they all shouted.

Rotty didn't know if he should wave back or run and hide, he had never seen anything quite so frightening as this thing that was spewing fire and flying.

'Don't be scared, Rotty,' the boys shouted. 'It's OK, it won't hurt you.'

Mr Jones brought the hot air balloon in to land, right next to where Rotty was standing.

'Wow,' the boys said, 'that was an adventure.'

'Nobody is ever going to believe us about flying,' said Toby-two.

'Nor about everything else that we have seen and done,' said Joshy-washy.

'This might help,' said Harry, as he put his hands into his rucksack and pulled out three small toy cars, two toy lorries, a helicopter and an aeroplane.

'Are you giving us these?' said Jay-pee.

'Yes, of course,' said Harry. 'It might make it easier for you to explain to everyone what you have seen. I have got lots of toys; I won't miss these.'

Rotty was still standing there with his mouth open.

'Close your mouth Rotty, you look like you're trying to catch flies,' they shouted.

The boys climbed out of the basket and Harry shook their hands. 'I have really enjoyed being with you,' he said. 'I hope it's not too long, before we see each other again.'

'It won't be,' they all promised.

Mr Jones was eager to get going. 'I want to get back, and get everything packed away before people start coming home from work,' he said.

'Thank you so much,' the boys told him. 'I don't know what we would have done without you,' said Joshy-washy, and the others agreed.

'That's OK,' he replied. 'I have enjoyed myself. I definitely want to come up into your world again, on a day when there is more time, so that I can have a look around. Maybe when Harry and Jane visit, I could bring them up in my balloon.'

'That would be fantastic,' said Toby-two.

'Can't wait,' agreed the others.

There was a roar from the flame, and the balloon took off. The boys stood there for ages waving, until it was completely out of sight.

'What an adventure we have had,' they told Rotty.

'What a telling off you are going to get,' he replied sternly. 'Do you know that everyone has been searching for you? I didn't know if I should tell them about going down the edge of the world or not, but decided to keep quiet.'

'We only went down again to fetch Plod. We forgot to bring him back when we went down with you, so we had to go down the following day to get him. We looked for you so we could tell you that we were going down again, but you were nowhere to be seen. Then after we found Plod – and that is a long story that we don't have time to tell you about today – we went back to the edge of the world to climb back up, and the ropes were missing. So there we were, stuck down in the other world.'

'I pulled the ropes up,' said Rotty. 'I didn't realise that you had gone down there again, and I thought that we had forgotten to pull them up the previous day. I knew that if anybody else saw the ropes, I would be in big trouble for a start. When everybody started searching for you, I didn't think for one minute that you were down in the other world, because the ropes were still coiled up, so I thought that you were exploring somewhere in Farbedrook, and didn't want to be found. Mumsy Kinnie-winkie is going to have your guts for garters when she sees you, and the girls and Granny Nellie are furious with you as well. You are not going to be let out to play for at least a week, maybe even longer.'

'When we are allowed out, we will come and see you to tell you all about everything that we saw,' promised Joshy-washy, 'but now I think that we had better go and face Mumsy Kinnie-winkie, so see you hopefully soon. Bye.'

The boys walked through Bedport Woods very slowly, not looking forward to being in trouble.

'Put the toys that Harry gave us in the bottom of your rucksack Jay-pee,' said Joshy-washy. 'I don't think that we ought to show Mumsy Kinnie-winkie or Granny Nellie them today.'

Chapter Seven

When the boys arrived home, everything was quiet. 'I wonder where the girls and Mumsy Kinnie-winkie are,' said Toby-two.

'Perhaps they are out looking for us still,' said Joshy-washy. 'I think that we ought to go upstairs and get changed into clean clothes, then get these dirty one washed.'

'Wouldn't it be good if we had one of those machines that Harry had, that you just put your dirty clothes in, and they came out clean,' said Toby-two.

'Yeah, and that other machine that dries it,' said Jay-pee.

'Well, we haven't,' said Joshy-washy, 'so we had better get washing and then hang them out in the garden to dry. If we do that, Mumsy Kinnie-winkie might not be quite so cross with us.'

The boys all did as Joshy-washy said. Afterwards they made themselves a sandwich, then went out to feed all of the animals.

While the boys were doing their washing in Farbed-rook, Mr Jones was pondering over in the other world. He had always believed that there were other worlds out there, and he felt honoured that he had played a part in getting the boys back to their world. The more he pondered the more he wanted to go back. He couldn't stop thinking when he was packing up his balloon.

Harry had stayed to help him, and he asked him who else apart from them, knew about the boys. Harry told him it was only Jane and the dog warden.

'Well, I think we had better keep it that way,' said Mr Jones. 'The dog warden has most probably for-gotten how different the boys and their dog looked, and if he did tell anyone they wouldn't take him seriously, as he drinks too much. People would just think that he had been on the booze again. In a couple of weeks, we will go up to the boys' world again, and have a really good look around. That man the boys called Rotty looked friendly enough. I know he looked extremely frightened of the balloon, but I expect the boys will tell him all about it, and then he will be only too pleased to welcome us. It was a brilliant idea of yours to give them those model cars. Chances are they will show them to quite a few people and hopefully those people will be very inquisitive about us,' said Mr Jones. 'Right then, Harry, let's go home. And remember, not a word to anyone except Jane.'

'OK,' said Harry, and they got into Mr Jones's truck to make their way back home.

Back in Farbedrook, the boys had only just finished seeing to the animals when Mumsy Kinnie-winkie came walking through the gate, with the girls. When they saw the boys, the girls came running over to them.

'Your in big, big trouble,' whispered Lottie.

Lu-lu put her arms round them and gave them a hug. Hanniepan burst into tears and threw herself into Jay-pee's arms.

'I thought that you were never coming back,' she cried, 'and then I wouldn't be a twin anymore, and I wouldn't like that.'

Jay-pee was secretly pleased that Hanniepan had missed him, but felt embarrassed that she was slobbering all over him.

'That's enough, Hanniepan,' he whispered. 'Let me go now.'

Mumsy Kinnie-winkie strode over to them.

'Do you know what you have put us all through?' she shouted at them.

'We thought that you had been eaten by something.'

'What on earth would eat us?' said Joshy-washy.

'I don't know, maybe a dragon or the lake monster,' said Mumsy Kinnie-winkie.

All the children began to giggle. 'There is no such thing as dragons,' laughed Lottie. 'Really, Mumsie Kinnie-winkie, I know that we were all worried where they had gone, but eaten by dragons – really!'

'Well, I was out of my mind with worry, anything could have happened to them. Now, you boys, straight after supper, you will go to your rooms, and each day for two weeks you will do extra chores.'

'Don't you want to know where we have been and what we have seen?' asked Toby-two.

'No,' replied Mumsy Kinnie-winkie. 'I most probably wouldn't believe you anyway, so I don't want to know.'

Joshy-washy leant over to Lottie. 'You girls come up to our rooms as soon as you can after supper; have we got things to show and tell you,' he whispered.

Chapter Eight

After the girls had helped to wash the dishes after supper; Mumsy Kinnie-winkie had gone over to Granny Nellie's house to tell her the boys had come home and to share some of her apple and nettle wine, so the girls made their way up to the boys' room.

The boys were playing with the toys that Harry had given them.

'What on earth are those?' said Lottie.

The boys started to tell them about going down the edge of the world and then having to go again because they had forgotten Plod. They told them about their new friends and the dog warden; about the bicycle, the helicopter, the car ride and all the funny gadgets in Harry's house: and last of all, about Mr Jones and his hot air balloon, and them all flying back up to Farbedrook in it.

'I don't believe a word of it,' said Hanniepan.

'I know it sounds unbelievable,' said Lottie, 'but if it's not true, where did they get these funny toys from?'

'I believe it,' said Lu-lu. 'Tell us more.'

The boys talked for hours about the adventure they'd had, and the girls listened intently.

'We are going to go again,' they told them, 'but before we do, Mr Jones is going to bring Harry and Jane up to Farbedrook, so that they can see our world. You will really like them, and if they like you, maybe they will invite you girls down to their world to see for yourself all the things we have told you about.'

'I can't wait,' said Lu-lu. 'Can we go tomorrow?'

'No, it will be a few weeks before we can go. Anyway, they are coming here first.'

'Jane is going to bring her old bicycle – the one that we all had a go on – to give to us, when she comes, as she is getting a new one for her birthday,' said Jay-pee.

'Is she just going to give it to us?' said Hanniepan.

'Yep,' replied Jay-pee.

The next morning the boys told the girls that they had to go and see Rotty.

'We are coming with you,' said Lottie. After they had done all their chores the children all ran through Bedport Woods to find Rotty.

As soon as they arrived at the row of trees near to the edge of the world, Rotty came out.

'You boys really scared me yesterday, arriving in that funny thing that flew.'

'Sorry you were scared, Rotty, but we have had such an adventure.' They sat on the ground and told him the whole story. The girls sat quietly listening as well, even though they had heard it all the night before.

'I am looking forward to them coming up here again,' said Rotty, 'but I don't think that we should tell anybody else yet.'

'Agreed,' said all the children.

The boys got out the toy cars, aeroplane and helicopter, and Rotty and the girls sat on the grass looking at them in wonder as the boys explained everything about them.

'It's time to go home,' said Lottie, always the sensible one. 'If we don't go soon, we will all be in trouble and kept in for a week.'

Rotty bid them goodbye and said he hoped that they would all come back to visit him soon.

'We will,' they all replied.

'And remember to bring those odd toys again,' he said.

The children walked back through the woods and got home, just before Mumsy Kinnie-winkie got in from visiting Old Man Disty-bun, with Granny Nellie.

'I hope that you have all behaved yourselves today,' she said.

'We have,' they all replied. 'We have just done our chores then went for a walk and played.'

As Mumsie Kinnie-winkie walked past them into the house, the children looked at each other with secret smiles.

Chapter Nine

As the boys lay in bed that night, their thoughts were on all that had happened to them in the last few days.

Toby-two, always the inquisitive one, suddenly said, 'Why doesn't anyone ever speak about our father? He went away just after the twins were born and nobody has ever mentioned him since.'

'Well, he can't still live in Farbedrook because if he did, we would bump into him.' replied Jay-pee.

Joshy-washy thought for a while then replied, 'I once asked Mumsie Kinnie-winkie where he was, when he had been gone for about a week, but I didn't get an answer. It was quite a long time ago and I wasn't very old, but I can still remember that there were lots of secret meetings at Grannie Nellie's house. Since then nobody has ever mentioned his name again, so I put it to the back of my mind.'

'I can't remember anything,' said Toby-two.

'Nor me,' said Jay-pee.

'Don't be so stupid!' said Joshy-washy. 'You were only

a tiny baby, so how would you remember anything?'

Jay-pee put his sulky face on and turned over in bed.

Toby-two started again, 'Why don't we go back to the edge of the world tomorrow and ask Rotty if he knows anything, I bet if he does, he will tell us.'

Hearing this, Jay-pee turned round to face them again, the sulky look on his face had been replaced by a smile. 'Go on Joshy-washy, please, it would be fun! I bet Rotty does know something. Please, please.'

Joshy-washy thought for a short while, 'OK,' he said. 'But you know that we promised the girls that they could come with us next time we went.'

'OK,' agreed the other two.

'Now, let's get some sleep,' said the ever sensible Joshy-washy, 'or we won't be going anywhere.'

The next morning, after all the chores were finished, the boys got the girls together and told them of their plan to go and visit Rotty, to see if they could find out anything about where their father had gone. Hanniepan started jumping up and down in excitement and Lu-lu nodded her head approvingly.

Lottie stood with her hands on her hips, thinking about it. 'OK, now listen to me. I am the eldest and what I say goes.'

Jay-pee made a face and whispered to Toby-two, 'Do we have to take her?' Toby-two giggled and Lottie whirled around.

'Did you say something?' Toby-two and Jay-pee put their most angelic looks on their faces and said that they were just laughing at Plod, because he was rolling around on the floor.

Lottie turned back to the others, 'As I was just saying before I was so rudely interrupted; I am the eldest and I will have to think about it.' The boys faces fell and Hanniepan stopped jumping; Lu-lu was just about to say something when Lottie looked at them all and laughed, 'Got you all, of course we will go, I can't wait!' Hanniepan started to jump up and down again and the others had to restrain her.

'Shush, Mumsie Kinnie-winkie hasn't gone out yet and she will come out to see what's going on,' said Lu-lu.

'Let's go in and ask for a picnic basket and then if we take the toof ball, nobody will suspect anything.' said Lottie.

Mumsie Kinnie-winkie was pleased that the children were going to play toof ball and quickly packed the picnic basket with goodies. She wanted to go round to see Grannie Nellie and if the children were going out, she need not hurry back.

With the picnic basket and toof ball in their hands, the children and Plod set out. Hanniepan kept running ahead, she was so excited. When they arrived in Bedport Woods, the children quickly ran through to the other side, past the warning sign, until they came to Rotty's house. Rotty was very pleased to see them; he had enjoyed himself more in the last few days than he ever had in his life before. The children sat down on the grass outside Rotty's house and started to ask him about their father. Rotty looked uncomfortable and turned his head away.

'You obviously know something.' said Lottie. 'Don't you think that you should tell us?'

Rotty looked at the children again and said that they had to promise not to tell anyone what he was about to tell them. The children all agreed and so Rotty began.

'The story began when I was a boy.' he said. 'Your grandfather was a very well respected man and he decided to go over the edge of the world. He took two friends with him, and the people of Farbedrook were all very excited to find out about what was down at the bottom. Parties were arranged for when the three brave men returned... but it never happened – they never came back.

The people of Farbedrook waited and waited, but after a few months had passed, they knew that something bad must have happened to them. Your father was always talking about it, and after you twins were born he took off on his own, to go over the edge and down into the other world and find his father. He left in the middle of the night so that nobody would try to stop him, just leaving a note to tell Mumsie Kinnie-winkie where he had gone, but like his father before him, he never returned. After that, new laws were made in Farbedrook, this house was erected near to the edge of the world and I was employed as the Keeper. The sign was put up warning people to keep away, and nobody has ever spoken about the missing people again. We are the only ones ever to have returned, and nobody must ever know that we went down.'

'So, my father and grandfather, who I have never met, are down there somewhere?' asked Hanniepan.

'I don't think so,' said Rotty. 'I think that something really bad must have happened to them.'

'But we know that the people that live in the world down there are very different and ugly, but they are not bad.' said Joshy-washy.

'I don't know what to think.' replied Rotty.

Lottie opened the picnic basket, 'Let's just have some lunch now and maybe we can think more about it after.' she said.

They all started to eat the sandwiches when suddenly Joshy-washy said, 'Where's Hanniepan?'

'Oh no,' said Lottie. 'I bet that she has gone to look at the edge of the world.' The children and Rotty immediately got up and started to run towards the trees that stood next to the edge of the world.

'I left the ropes tied to the trees,' Rotty shouted. 'She wouldn't attempt to go down them, would she?'

As they arrived at the edge they saw that one of the ropes had been let down, they looked over and saw Hanniepan sliding down the rope.

'Hanniepan, come back!' they all shouted.

Hanniepan shouted back, 'I'm going to find my father and grandfather,' and carried on sliding down the rope.

'Oh well,' said the boys with smiles on their faces, as they jumped onto the ropes and started to slide down, 'are you coming Rotty?'

'Don't forget us!' chorused the girls and all the children plus Rotty holding Plod under one of his arms, started to slide down.

'Here we go again...' they called out as they all slid down the rope into their next adventure.

The End

Printed in the United Kingdom by
Lightning Source UK Ltd., Milton Keynes
136915UK00001B/190-264/P